RUBY'S REVENGE

LUNCH ROOM
BE NEAT

RUBY'S REVENGE

by
Cheryl Pelavin

G. P. Putnam's Sons • New York

Published simultaneously in
Canada by Longmans Canada Limited, Toronto.
Library of Congress Catalog Card Number: 76-185403
SBN GB-399-60776-5
PRINTED IN THE UNITED STATES OF AMERICA
04208

One day in school Ruby the skunk was taking a spelling test.

Alice the porcupine poked Ruby and whispered, “How do you spell ‘eggplant’?”

Ruby opened her mouth to tell Alice that she didn't know, when Mrs. Sidoti, the teacher, yelled, "Ruby gets a zero for talking during a test!" *Boy,* muttered Ruby, *I wish Alice would just disappear!*

When the test was over and it was time for lunch, Ruby looked everywhere for Alice, but couldn't find her. *Maybe I did make her disappear,* thought Ruby.

So Ruby sat down next to Barbara the armadillo. Barbara always had a tuna on rye for lunch. Ruby never liked her own lunch, so she asked Barbara to trade bites. Barbara said, “No.” Ruby said, “You know what? I wish you’d disappear too!”

When she looked up from her sandwich, Barbara was gone. So Ruby finished Barbara's tuna on rye and thought, *I wonder if I really can make people disappear.*

After lunch Mrs. Sidoti yelled at the whole class, and especially Ruby, for being noisy. Ruby shut her eyes and concentrated very hard. *I wish, I wish that Mrs. Sidoti would disappear!*

When Ruby opened her eyes, there was no more rhinoceros! Ruby was stunned. The rest of the class started to pass notes and talk and throw things.

Ruby was thinking about who to make disappear next when Bert the chipmunk passed her a note. "Thank you!" said Ruby. "It's not for *you*," said Bert. "It's for Karen from Stanley." "Is that so?? Well why don't *you* disappear," said Ruby.

Ruby was about to pass the note when Karen snatched it out of her paw and said, “Thank you, Ruby.” Ruby just smiled and said, “I wish you’d disappear also,” and the white cat did.

Then Ruby went over to Stanley.

"Would you like to play with me after school?" Stanley laughed and said, "You?" Ruby said, "I guess you won't because you won't be here, BECAUSE I WISH YOU'D DISAPPEAR TOO!" And he did.

There were no more classmates left except Rhoda. Rhoda was an aardvark who was always getting in the way. She came up to Ruby and said, "Will you be my best friend?" Ruby just sighed and said, "Oh, Rhoda, you might as well disappear too." And Rhoda disappeared, very quietly.

Ruby was alone! She flew to the blackboard. She drew flowers and pictures of everyone in the class. And then she drew a big rhinoceros.

She used up all the colored chalk and all the white chalk. She had a wonderful time because drawing on the blackboard was strictly forbidden.

Then she erased the whole thing. She used big wet sponges. This was forbidden also except for the blackboard monitor.

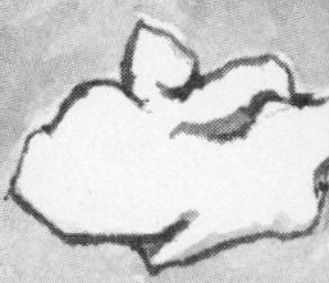

Then Ruby ran around and watered the palm tree and the kangaroo vine and the avocado tree. Ruby was never chosen to be the watering monitor either.

Then Ruby found the grade book. Her name was listed: Skunk, Ruby. With a red pencil she changed all her 0's to 100's.

Then she stood in front of the class and told everyone what a wonderful skunk she was. "I have all 100's in my book!" she yelled.

"And I can draw all over the blackboard if I want to!

“And water all the plants!

"And I can make anyone I want disappear!"

Then she marched back to her seat and sat down. It was very quiet. She waited for someone to come and ask her what she got on her spelling test. But no one did.

She waited for someone to pass her a note. But no one did. No one did anything. NO ONE WAS THERE.

"This is even worse than before," she moaned. "What good is it being great all by myself? What fun is it getting to do everything if nobody's watching?" She put her head down on her desk and cried. "I wish everybody would come back." She wished so hard she fell asleep.

"Ruby, get your head up off that desk and sit up straight!" screamed Mrs. Sidoti.

Ruby woke up. She was so mad at Mrs. Sidoti she was about to wish *you know what* when something told her not to. Instead, she decided to give them all a second chance.

For the time being, anyway.